DAMIAN DROOTH SUPERSLEUTH

THE CASE OF THE POP STAR'S WEDDING

by Barbara Mitchelhill

illustrated by Tony Ross

Librarian Reviewer
Marci Peschke
Librarian, Dallas Independent School District
M.A. Education Reading Specialist, Stephen F. Austin State University
Learning Resources Endorsement, Texas Women's University

Reading Consultant
Elizabeth Stedem
Educator/Consultant, Colorado Springs, CO
M.A. in Elementary Education, University of Denver, CO

STONE ARCH BOOKS
Minneapolis   San Diego

First published in the United States in 2007
by Stone Arch Books,
151 Good Counsel Drive, P.O. Box 669,
Mankato, Minnesota 56002.
www.stonearchbooks.com

First published in 2002
by Andersen Press Ltd, London.

Library of Congress Cataloging-in-Publication Data
Mitchelhill, Barbara.
    The Case of the Pop Star's Wedding / by Barbara Mitchelhill; illustrated
by Tony Ross.
    p. cm. — (Pathway Books) (Damian Drooth Supersleuth)
    Summary: Young detective Damian Drooth insists on going along when
his mother is hired to cater his favorite pop singer's wedding reception, and
it proves fortunate that he is there when he witnesses the theft of a diamond
necklace.
    ISBN-13: 978-1-59889-118-8 (hardcover)
    ISBN-10: 1-59889-118-9 (hardcover)
    ISBN-13: 978-1-59889-268-0 (paperback)
    ISBN-10: 1-59889-268-1 (paperback)
    [1. Weddings—Fiction. 2. Robbers and outlaws—Fiction. 3. Singers—
Fiction. 4. Mystery and detective stories.] I. Ross, Tony, ill. II. Title.
III. Series. IV. Series: Pathway books V. Series: Mitchelhill, Barbara.
Damian Drooth Supersleuth.
PZ7.M697Casp 2007
[Fic]—dc22   2006007178

Art Director: Heather Kindseth
Graphic Designer: Kay Fraser

1 2 3 4 5 6 11 10 09 08 07 06

Printed in the United States of America.

Table of Contents

Chapter 1

My name is Drooth. Damian Drooth. Crime buster and ace detective.

So when Mom got a letter, I read it.

Dear Mrs. Drooth,

I was wondering if you would be interested in providing the food for my wedding. Perhaps you could come to see me and discuss the menu.

Yours sincerely,

Tiger Lilly

I stared at the name. I was shocked.

"Tiger Lilly?" I yelled. (It was hard to stay calm.) "The singer? One of the Bay Babes?"

Mom nodded and my head exploded. Tiger Lilly was my favorite singer ever! I was her number one fan! Wow! Wow! Wow!

That morning, Mom called Tiger Lilly and arranged a meeting.

"I'll come with you," I said.

"I don't think so," said Mom as she wrote the date in her planner.

"You might get lost," I insisted.

"I can read a map, Damian."

"I could be your secretary and take notes for you."

"I don't want a secretary."

"Fine! I'll go on a hunger strike if you don't take me!" I threatened.

Mom sighed. "Don't be silly, Damian!" she said. "No!"

In the end, she gave in. My mom's brain power is no match for my razor-sharp smarts.

And so I got to meet the amazing Tiger Lilly.

Chapter 2

Tiger Lilly's place was huge! The driveway was longer than my street.

As we pulled up outside the front door, there she was, waiting for us on the steps. A star! Some guys would have gone wild. But not me! Fame doesn't bother me. Even though her eyes were deep blue and her hair was blonde and hung down to her waist, I stayed cool.

Then Mom spoke. "This is my little boy, Damian," she said in her mommy voice. "I hope you don't mind that he came with me. There was no one home to watch him, and he gets into trouble when he's alone."

I was so embarrassed.

But I stuffed my hands in my pockets and just said, "Hi!" as if I met celebrities every day.

We followed Tiger Lilly down the hall and into a fantastic room with big comfy chairs and a giant fireplace.

"Well, Damian," she said, as she poured us some tea, "I've got a little brother and he's always getting into trouble, too!"

"It may seem like trouble to some," I said, "but the fact is I work undercover. I'm a private eye."

I could see she was very impressed.

"I track down crooks, bank robbers, forgers . . . that kind of thing," I added.

Tiger Lilly turned and looked at Mom.

"You didn't tell me you had your own detective agency, Mrs. Drooth!" she said.

Then she winked at me — or maybe she had something in her eye. "He'll be useful on the day of the wedding. I don't want any of my presents getting stolen!"

Mom looked scared. "Oh, Damian won't be here on your wedding day."

"I wouldn't want him here with all your guests around. He'd just get in the way."

I couldn't believe it! After all the times I've helped Mom out!

Okay, so I've broken a couple of dishes. But I was still her most trusted helper! I deserved to go!

Luckily, Tiger Lilly insisted that I should be there. "You organize the food, Mrs. Drooth, and Damian can keep a lookout for suspicious characters."

I couldn't believe it. I had been employed as a private detective at the wedding of the year!

Chapter 3

It was three weeks before the wedding. I needed to sharpen up my detective skills. In my notebook, I had a detective idea to help me in my work:

Anyone whose eyes were very close together should not be trusted.

But one idea wasn't enough. I decided to spend some time studying detective stories. There were some great ones in my comics.

Mom didn't understand, of course. "Why can't you read a real book?" she said. Shows what she knows.

After ten days of serious study, I came up with a new theory, or idea: Anyone with a beard (particularly a dark one) is probably up to no good.

Working out an idea is one thing.
Proving it is another. This is how I did it.

Monday

Our teacher, Mr. Grimethorpe, is sick.
They say it's stress. But how can that
be? Teachers have it so easy! If you ask
me, he spends too much time shouting and
thumping his desk.

Our new teacher is Mr. Symes, who has a beard!

Tuesday

Mr. Symes really likes money. He counts our lunch money twice. He needs to be watched.

Wednesday

9:15 Mr. Symes counts field trip money three times!!!!!!

9:30 Mr. Symes puts money in his briefcase. This proves he is a thief.

9:35 Work out plan in back of math book.

9:45 Put plan into action. Stuff briefcase under my sweater. Creep out of classroom when M.S. isn't looking.

9:50 Go to find Mrs. Frank, our school secretary.

10:00 School office locked. No sign of Mrs. Frank. Probably making coffee and chocolate cookies for the principal.

10:10 Hide briefcase in locker room. Will pick it up later.

10:15 Go back to class. M.S. has a terrible temper. He makes me stay in at recess for no reason. He is a real criminal for sure.

11:00 Police arrive. How do they know about the money? M.S. looks worried.

No wonder!

Thursday

9:00 No sign of Mr. Symes. I guess he's in prison. I will not mention my part in his downfall to the police.

See? My theory about the beard was proved. Now I could track down any criminal who dared to go to Tiger Lilly's wedding.

Chapter 4

On the morning of the wedding, Mom was nervous. But I had my notebook and my pen, and I was ready to take on the big names of the underworld, if necessary.

"Damian!" Mom shouted. "Don't stand there in a daze. Help me get these desserts into the van."

Does James Bond carry desserts for his mom? No! But that day, Mom was in a bad mood. So I picked up a big chocolate mousse and carried it as carefully as I could.

It was not my fault that the path was uneven. It was not my fault that I slipped.

Mom didn't speak to me on the way to Tiger Lilly's place. She just gripped the wheel and frowned at the road ahead. She was in a terrible mood.

When we reached the house, there was a security man on the gate. He was huge and wore a badge that said **Dean**. I was surprised that Tiger Lilly had hired him when she knew I was coming.

Mom stopped and rolled down the window. "Catering," she said.

"I need to see your passes," said Dean.

Mom handed her card out the window. I leaned over and flashed the detective badge I had made the night before. We were waved straight in. No big deal.

On the lawn in front of Tiger Lilly's house was a gigantic tent.

There were tons of people around, carrying chairs and arranging flowers. Mom parked the van behind the tent and started unloading the food. She was dashing backward and forward like a wild thing, carrying trays and dishes. She got really out of breath.

I offered to help but she said she'd rather do it herself. "All right," I said. "I'll go and look around for crooks."

Mom gave me one of her looks. "Don't you dare get into trouble!" she shouted over a pile of cookies. "I've got enough to think about without worrying about you."

"Stay cool!" I said. "I'm in control!'

It wasn't long before I saw a man who was very suspicious. He was wearing a black suit with a white shirt and was carrying a black leather case.

Spooky! And guess what? His eyes were really close together. (Detective Theory number 1.) If that wasn't enough, he had a black beard, too! (Detective Theory number 2.)

I had hit the jackpot! This man was a criminal for sure. I did a quick sketch of him and made some notes in my notebook.

Then I followed him into the house. It was obvious he was planning to steal the wedding presents.

Chapter 5

I walked behind him with my back pressed against the wall, just like detectives on TV. But, before I got close, somebody shouted, "Hey, kid!" and a security guard grabbed me by the collar.

"What do you think you're doing in here?" he asked me.

I looked at his badge (which said **Curt**) and showed him mine. "I'm with Mom's catering company," I said.

Curt grunted.

"I'm Tiger Lilly's personal protection officer," I said.

Curt laughed! What was so funny? "Out you go, sonny," he said, as if I was a little kid. "Go find your mom."

Of course, I didn't. I owed it to Tiger Lilly to watch over her presents. I walked away, pretending to head for the tent. When I was sure that Curt was gone, I hurried back toward the house and sneaked down the side.

I peeked in through a window and saw the presents spread out on a table. Each one had a label showing who had sent it.

There were lots of silver plates and cups. There were old paintings that must have been worth at least a million dollars, too.

In the middle of it all was a fantastic diamond necklace.

A large label said, "To Tiger Lilly on our wedding day, from Gary with love and kisses." Yuck!

Tiger Lilly was marrying Gary Blaze. I didn't know why. He was a soccer player with skinny legs and no hair. He was terrible at everything except scoring goals.

Why did Tiger Lilly fall for someone like that? She needed a guy with super brainpower. Someone who could spot a crook a mile away.

As I looked through the window, the man with the beard walked into the room. He stared at the necklace.

It was obvious that he was going to take it when the not-very-smart security guard (**Curt**) wasn't looking.

I worked out a plan. I ran around to the front door, hid behind some vines, and waited.

Ten minutes later the man in black came out and I followed him down the path. He stopped, looked at his watch, and started running toward the tent.

I thought it was very strange.

But I was onto him.

By that time, the reception was in full swing. The crook went to the back of the tent, lifted a loose flap, and sneaked in. He was smart, all right! But he wasn't going to get away.

I hurried to the main entrance of the tent. Inside, everybody was eating and talking. I could see Tiger Lilly, who looked pretty in a long white dress with flowers in her hair and silver nail polish. Gary Blaze looked dumb in a blue suit. (What did she see in him?)

I looked around, trying to spot the thief. I spotted him hiding with the band. He was pretending to play a saxophone.

If he thought he would get away with the necklace, he was making a big mistake!

Chapter 6

I had to tell Tiger Lilly what was going on. I started running toward her but before I could get close, a hand landed on my shoulder and a security guard (**Kelvin**) grabbed me.

I yelled but nobody came to help. They were too busy stuffing themselves with Mom's food.

"What do you think you're doing?" said Kelvin as he dragged me outside.

I started to explain. "I'm tracking down . . ."

But before I could finish, Curt came dashing out of the big house shouting, "Come here, Kelvin! Quick!"

Kelvin dropped me like a hot potato and ran toward Curt.

I followed them, of course. Something was up, and I was on the trail!

"The diamond necklace has been stolen," said Curt.

"I know that," I said, just trying to be helpful.

The guards turned and looked at me. "How do you know?" said Kelvin.

"I'm a private eye," I said, holding out my badge.

They raised their eyebrows and smirked. But I ignored them. "I was watching the presents when I saw someone take the necklace."

(It was nearly true. I didn't actually see him take it. But I almost saw him. It couldn't have been anyone else, could it?)

I flicked open my supersleuth notebook and found the right page.

"The thief was a tall, thin male with a beard, wearing a black suit, a white shirt, and carrying a black case."

They looked at me as if I'd crawled out from under a stone.

"Silly kid!" said Curt. "That's Dave. He plays in the band!"

I smiled. "Just a cover for his criminal activities," I said.

"I bet the necklace is in his case."

They snorted and pushed me to one side.

"Call the police, Curt," said Kelvin. "Don't tell any of the guests or the wedding will be ruined."

Curt got out his cell phone and dialed 911.

"As for you!" said Kelvin, turning to me. "I thought we sent you back to your mother."

He didn't let me explain. He slung me over his shoulder like a sack of carrots. I couldn't believe it!

I thought he'd take me to the refreshment tent. But he didn't. He took me to Mom's van.

"Okay!" he said, swinging open the back door. "You can stay there until your mom's finished with the food. Then she can take care of you." He flung me inside and slammed the door shut.

I didn't have the energy to try to escape. Suddenly I felt weak. My brain was slowing down. I knew it was the stress of chasing criminals, and my lack of food. Luckily, I spotted a chocolate cake in the back of the van. It's one of my favorites. So I had a slice, in the interest of crime detection.

Remember this tip: Chocolate cake is excellent for energy. I felt so much better after one slice that I had another. The more I ate, the more my brainpower increased. It was amazing! I hid the plate so Mom wouldn't notice the missing cake. I didn't want her to get upset.

Now I was ready for action. Escaping would be no problem. You see, the lock on the van door was broken.

When Mom locked it up at night, she had to put a chain around the handles. She said it was cheaper than buying a new lock.

But the guard didn't know that, did he? He thought he'd locked me in. Tee hee!

Slowly, I opened the door and peeked out. I was a few feet from the entrance of the tent.

I could see Tiger Lilly (still looking great), and the band on the far side. But there were security guards everywhere. It would be almost impossible to get in without being seen.

So how could I reach the thief and
save the diamond necklace?

Chapter 7

Being a trained detective, I soon had the problem figured out.

Between the van and the entrance was a large cart with the wedding cake on top. Perfect! All I had to do was distract the waiter.

Then I would hide under the cart.

"Excuse me!" I said, climbing out of the van.

"Somebody's looking for you. I can hear them shouting over there," I said.

The waiter looked puzzled, but went off around the back of the van where I had pointed. That was my chance. I dashed over, lifted the cloth from the cart, and slipped into the bottom of the cart.

The waiter was back in no time.

"Hmmph! Kids!" I heard him mutter. "Always up to their tricks!"

Then he pushed the cart into the tent, across the wooden floor, and stopped in front of the bride's table. Everybody cheered and clapped as Tiger Lilly and the bald soccer player walked toward it to cut the cake.

That's when I leaped out.

"Hold everything!" I shouted. (I once heard a detective say this in a movie. I thought it sounded good.)

"Stand clear!" I added, just for good measure. "There is a crook in here, and he's stolen a diamond necklace!"

I must admit, I was surprised Tiger Lilly didn't rush to my side.

Hadn't she understood what I said?

Instead, security guards were running toward me from every corner of the tent like crazy gorillas.

I jumped back onto the cart.

Pushing off with one foot, I skimmed over the floor toward the band.

"The one with the saxophone!" I shouted. "The necklace is hidden in his black case!"

At this point, the cart ran out of control and smashed into the band. I whizzed through the air like Superman and landed on the stage, while the cake shot across the floor, leaving behind a lake of white frosting.

I stared up into the face of the crook. (His beard looked even worse close up.)

"Gotcha!" I said.

But it was the man behind him who suddenly jumped off the stage and made a run for it. Unluckily for him, he skidded on the puddle of frosting. His feet flew out from under him and he fell on his back like a beached whale.

Meanwhile, I climbed across the stage and reached into his case.

"I think he's forgotten something," I called out.

I held up the necklace for all to see. Everybody was on their feet.

They stood in a huge circle around the crook, pushing and shoving to get a better look.

Then the police arrived.

"What's going on?" said the inspector. "Have you caught the thief?"

"Thanks to this boy, we have," said Tiger Lilly.

"This is Damian Drooth, and he could teach the police a thing or two about solving crimes."

As she spoke, she put her arm around my shoulder.

I almost fainted with pride.

Chapter 8

I guess you're wondering how I managed to track down the jewel thief. After all, he didn't have a beard like my first suspect.

Well, I must admit there was a little mistake.

You see, I don't know the names of musical instruments.

So when I shouted, "It's the one with the saxophone!" I got it wrong. I should have said it was the man with the trumpet. I got them mixed up.

This is a trumpet:

And this is a saxophone:

But it didn't matter.

As it turned out, the man who stole the necklace really was playing the saxophone. Lucky mistake, huh?

As for Tiger Lilly, she was thrilled I'd stopped the crook.

I asked her if she'd sign my CDs.

She said, "Oh Damian, I'll give you a copy of every CD I've ever made and sign them for you."

Then she kissed me on the cheek. That was a little girly for me, but it was okay, really.

Gary Blaze came over and said, "Thanks a lot, Damian." I think he's a wimp. He said he'd give me a soccer ball and he'd sign it for me.

But I said, "No thanks. I'm not really into soccer."

Everybody cheered for me and they made a big deal. They asked me what I would like to eat and made me sit at one of the fancy tables.

"Sorry, Damian," said Kelvin when he brought me two plates of food. "We ran out of chocolate cake. Will strawberries be okay?"

It's the thought that counts.

When everything had calmed down and most of the police were gone, Inspector Crockitt came over to me.

I've met him before. Sometimes he tries to pick up tips on solving crimes.

"How did you catch him, Damian?" he asked.

I'm too modest to tell a police inspector how to do his job. But I do like to help.

"Well, I have this theory about beards," I said.

"Is that how you solved this case?" he asked.

I could see he really wanted to know.

"Maybe," I said, winking at him. "But maybe I got lucky."

They don't call me Supersleuth for nothing.

About the Author

Barbara Mitchelhill started writing when she was seven years old. She says, "When I was eight or nine, I used to pretend I was a detective, just like Damian. My friend, Liz, and I used to watch people walking down our street and we would write clues in our notebooks. I don't remember catching any criminals!" She has written many books for children. She lives in Shropshire, England, and gets some of her story ideas when she walks her dogs, Jeff and Ella.

About the Illustrator

Tony Ross was born in London in 1938. He has illustrated lots of books, including some by Paula Danziger, Michael Palin, and Roald Dahl. He also writes and illustrates his own books. He has worked as a cartoonist, graphic designer, and art director of an advertising agency. When he was a kid, he wanted to grow up to be a cowboy.

Glossary

catering (KAY-tur-ing)—providing with food

celebrities (suh-LEB-ruh-teez)—famous people

daze (DAYZ)—a condition when you cannot think clearly

detective (di-TEK-tiv)—someone whose work is solving crimes

forger (FORJ-ur)—someone who makes illegal copies of things, such as CDs, DVDs, or paintings

hunger strike (HUHNG-ur STRIKE)—to choose to not eat as a way to protest

pride (PRIDE)—feeling good about oneself

sleuth (SLOOTH)—a detective

suspicious (suh-SPISH-uhss)—thinking or feeling that something is wrong

theory (THEER-ee)—an idea or belief

underworld (UHN-dur-wurld)—people that are organized for the purpose of crime

Discussion Questions

1. Damian comes up with a few ideas about identifying suspicious characters. Discuss his theories and talk about whether or not they are true. Do you think his theories would work catching criminals in real life?

2. At the end of the story, why does Damian nearly faint with pride?

4. Damian keeps running into security guards. Why do you think there are so many guards at Tiger Lilly's wedding?

Writing Prompts

1. Imagine meeting a famous celebrity. Write a story about who you would like to meet and what would happen when you did meet him/her.

2. Can you make up a case for Damian to solve? Write about it.

3. How do you detect a suspicious character? Describe three of your theories and how you came up with them.

Internet Sites

Do you want to know more about subjects related to this book? Or are you interested in learning about other topics? Then check out FactHound, a fun, easy way to find Internet sites.

Our investigative staff has already sniffed out great sites for you!

Here's how to use FactHound:

1. Visit *www.facthound.com*

2. Select your grade level.

3. To learn more about subjects related to this book, type in the book's ISBN number: **1598891189**.

4. Click the **Fetch It** button.

FactHound will fetch the best Internet sites for you!